6TH GRADE REVENGERS 1

CAT CRIMES AND WANNABES

STEVEN WHIBLEY

Published by Steven Whibley Publishing
Victoria, British Columbia
www.stevenwhibley.com

Editing: Maya Packard
Copyediting: Chandler Groover
Cover Design: Pintado (rogerdespi.8229@gmail.com)
Interior Layout and Design: Tammy Desnoyers (www.tammydesign.ca)

Library and Archives Canada Cataloguing in Publication

Whibley, Steven, 1978-, author
Cat crimes and wannabes / Steven Whibley.

(6th grade revengers ; 1)
Issued in print and electronic formats.
ISBN 978-1-927905-08-1 (paperback).--ISBN 978-1-927905-07-4 (pdf)

I. Title.

PS8645.H46C38 2015 jC813'.6 C2015-905579-2
C2015-905580-6

For Isaiah and Aubree

– Steven Whibley

CHAPTER 1

My sister Sky wrapped her arms around my legs, squeezing me like a boa constrictor.

"Sky, get behind the bed," I whispered, trying to unglue her from my body.

She shook her head and looked up at me through the darkness. Her lip quivered. "What if he gets past you? What if he gets me?"

"He won't," I whispered. "Now stop talking and go behind your bed. Don't come out until I say."

She hesitated for a second and then darted away. A moment later, her curly brown hair and huge green eyes peeked up over the edge of her bed.

Okay, I told myself, *let's do this*.

I shimmied along the wall toward Sky's closet door, which was cracked open the smallest bit. I raised my knife, ready to stab whatever I found inside. At the edge of the closet door, I took a deep breath, ready to throw my life down in order to save my little sister. Gripping my knife, I reached out with my free hand. With one quick motion, I yanked open the door and threw myself into the closet.

“Hai-ya!” I yelled as I slashed into the darkness like a maniac. Boxes of shoes and Barbie dolls tumbled down from the shelves, knocking me in the side of my face. I stumbled back and stepped on a ball made of nails, or at least that’s what it felt like. I yelped and fell flat on my back.

My sister lost it as only a six-year-old girl could. Her scream ricocheted around the room. I didn’t have much time—I had to kill the beast before anyone else charged into the room. Jumping up, I dove back into the closet. I shoved my knife deep into the wardrobe and twisted.

“Aha!”

A moment later I walked out of the closet, my hands over

my head in victory.

Sky clambered up from behind her bed and bounced toward me, her arms as wide as the smile on her face. She smashed into me just as Dad burst into the room. I caught her, but the impact forced me back a step and my foot landed again on her stupid toy. The two of us collapsed on the floor.

"What in the world is going on in here?" Dad asked, staring down at us. "Is that a knife, Jared?" He took it from my hand and flicked the blade with his thumb. It was rubber and had come with a Halloween costume I'd used a couple years ago. But it was perfect for what I was killing that particular night.

Sky jumped up and wrapped her arms around my dad. "He killed him, Daddy," she shouted. "Jared killed the bogeyman!"

My dad looked from Sky to me to the closet. I sat rubbing my foot. Dad seemed to put things together. "Did he?"

Sky nodded. "He stabbed him." She made stabbing movements with her hand toward the closet, which was actually a pretty creepy thing to see a little girl do.

Dad glanced at me with raised eyebrows. "Say goodnight to your brother, Sky. Let's get you back to bed."

There was a spy movie I'd been wanting to watch, so I bolted from the room, only to find my older sister, Ronie, watching some reality show while she stretched. She was in gymnastics and it seemed like she was always stretching. She taught gymnastics in order to pay for gymnastics and saved what little she had left over. Her dream was to train with Maxim Gorelov, the great

Russian Olympian, but he was outrageously expensive.

Ronie grinned when she saw me. "Sounded like you did pretty good in there. Killed the bogeyman, eh? A regular assassin." She got a good laugh at that.

I was about to hit her with a snappy comeback but I heard the door to Sky's room close. My dad's footsteps clunked down the hall. Stepping into the living room, he put his hands on his hips and looked at me very carefully. "For the past two weeks your mother and I have been trying to teach Sky there is no bogeyman and she doesn't need to be afraid of anything."

"Dad, I know, but—"

He held up his hand, cutting me off. "Your little sister just went to bed with a smile on her face, certain the bogeyman would never bother her again—or anyone else, for that matter." He tossed me a quarter. "She wanted you to have that. Payment for ridding her room of that spooky beast."

"Ha!" Ronie said. "Look at you. Getting paid for saving little girls from imaginary monsters."

Dad put his hand on my shoulder. "Jared, as much as I want your sister to not believe in spooky things that aren't real, I have to admit that what you did was very sweet. So thank you."

His cell phone rang. Pulling it from his pocket, he walked away to answer it.

"Lucky," Ronie said. "If that little stunt had backfired—if you'd made Sky more afraid of monsters under her bed—you'd have been grounded for sure."

"In her closet."

"Huh?"

"The monster. It wasn't under her bed, it was in the closet."

Ronie shrugged and turned back to the TV. "Jared Moter, Destroyer of Closet Monsters," she said in her fake-movie-preview voice. "Wait," she added, "why stop there? Maybe someone wants to get revenge on their imaginary friend for not sharing their imaginary toys."

"You're hilarious," I said.

"Jared Moter," she called as I headed toward my room, "Exactor of Revenge on All Things Imaginary."

I stepped into my room and closed the door. Ronie was a royal pain, but that night her words tumbled around inside my head. *Exactor of Revenge on All Things Imaginary.* I'm sure it was just a combination of feeling good about helping Sky and thinking about the spy movie I wanted to watch, but the more I thought about it, the more I liked the idea.

I sat at my desk and looked up at the poster on my wall from the spy museum in Washington, D.C. My school went on a class trip there last year and the spy museum was the highlight of the trip. The Lincoln Memorial was great and all that but learning about international and domestic spy rings, spy gadgets, and the life of lies every spy must live made me realize that *that* was what I wanted to do with my life. When I got back home I did some research and found out there's an actual spy camp for kids right near us in southern California. When I told Marcus about it he was all in. And we were ready to go until our parents told us we'd have to pay for it ourselves.

I looked at the quarter Sky had given me, thinking.

One of my favorite TV shows was about a spy who couldn't be a real spy anymore so he went around helping people with their problems. In a way, that was exactly what I'd done for Sky. She had a problem, and I fixed it. I wasn't sure what that would be called, but there had to be thousands of people with problems—problems like evil bosses, jerk teachers or pain-in-the-butt sisters—who needed someone to help them deal.

Someone like me.

I grabbed a notebook and pencil and started brainstorming all the ways I'd make it work. Eventually my brainstorm became a brain typhoon, or whatever it is when your imagination gets out of control. Brain tornado maybe. The ideas came faster than I could write them down. There was no limit to what I could do. Bullies would disappear from playgrounds. Mean babysitters would never sit again. The possibilities seemed endless.

Pretty soon it was after midnight and I had a notebook filled with ideas.

"Jared Moter: Avenger of the Little Guy," I said to myself as I crawled into bed. No, *avenger* wouldn't work. That was already a comic book and a movie. Revenge-inator? That sounded like a robot from a sci-fi movie. It had to be cool. Had to be catchy. "Problem Assassin?" I shook my head. I wasn't really killing stuff and besides, assassins were cool in movies and video games but not in real life.

I lay there staring up at the ceiling for a long time. Just before I fell asleep, I found the right word.

Revenger.

I said the word out loud and smiled. Yeah, that worked. I liked that. I could even make business cards—though I wasn't sure people who helped settle scores had business cards. *One step at a time*, I told myself. But I was definitely on to something.

CHAPTER 2

The next day I walked Sky to school like always. The air was crisp and cool, perfect September weather. We waited at the corner for my best friend, Marcus, and luckily he was on time and we left before Ronie. Ronie's school was right across the street from ours, but she walked alone or with her friends. It wasn't that I hated walking with her. Ronie can actually be semi-cool every so often, but lately—like today—her loser boyfriend, Gunner, walked her to school.

Luckily, my buddy Marcus was on time, so we managed to head to school before Gunner showed up. As Sky skipped ahead of us after a bogeyman-free sleep, I told Marcus what had happened and about my business idea.

"I don't get it," he said. "I mean, I get why you were in the closet, but I don't understand why you stabbed your sister's clothes."

"I was stabbing the bogeyman! But that's not the point of the story. The point is, I think I could do this for other people. Deal with their problems, you know. Like if they want someone dealt with, I could deal with them."

"Did your sister think he was wearing her clothes? What kind of monster does she think the bogeyman is?"

"Would you forget about the bogeyman, please? I think I'm on to something here."

"A business of eliminating imaginary monsters who wear little girls' dresses?"

"Forget the dresses already!"

"Okay, fine. What exactly is it you think you'd take on?"

"Anything. Anyone." I watched Sky to make sure she stopped at the intersection. Of course she did. "Think about it: someone's making your life miserable, or maybe you're getting beat up at school every day and don't want to go to the principal. Or maybe someone scammed you out of some money, or you have a cheating boyfriend. You contact me, and I deal with them for you."

"Like payback? Like...oh! You got served!"

"I came up with a name..."

"And that name would be?"

I hesitated. Marcus would either love it or he'd laugh and I'd feel stupid for thinking it up.

"C'mon, Jared, spill already. As long as it doesn't have to do with monsters in dresses, I'm sure it's not that bad."

"The Revengers," I blurted, and before Marcus could say anything I added, "Like a combination of avenger and revenge."

He smiled, and I thought he was going to laugh, but instead he said, "I like it."

"You do?"

"Yeah," he said. "Okay, so what else would you do?"

We'd made it to school by then. It was still early so we all sat on the steps. Sky sat next to me and colored in her notebook. I pulled out my notebook and handed it to Marcus. "Look at what I came up with."

He took the book and leafed through the pages. After minute his smile widened. "Dude, this could totally work."

"That's what I've been saying."

"You're going to need a partner." He wiggled his eyebrows at me.

"Well, duh. That's why I'm talking to you."

His smile widened. "Naturally." He closed the notebook and handed it back. "Okay, I'm in. But I need seventy percent of the profits."

"Fifty-fifty," I said, stuffing the book back in my bag.

"Sixty-forty." He put out his hand.

"It's fifty-fifty or you're my first target," I said, shaking his hand. "Not only can we practice our skills but we'll earn money for our spy camp fund. Win all around."

"This is going to be awesome." Marcus's face fell suddenly, and I turned around just in time to see Gunner and Ronie walking toward us.

"Hey, if it isn't the dork patrol," Gunner said.

Gunner. Even his name made me cringe. He was a total waste of space and treated Ronie like garbage. I think the only reason she liked him was because he was a couple years older—he'd graduated high school the previous year—and her friends thought he was hot.

Gunner didn't go to college and didn't have a job. All he did was ride around on his ten-speed with his guitar on his back. He had a car, but it was a scrap heap, and he rarely drove it if he had to go farther than from his house to ours. I'm pretty sure the car would choke and die if it had to go any farther. Basically, the guy was a textbook loser who played video games and pretended to write songs all day long. Sadly, he did both of those things at my house, which might not have been too bad except for the fact that he sounded a lot like a cat stuck in a garbage can when he sang.

"Hey, little bit," Gunner said to Sky, ruffling her hair. She ducked her head away from his hand.

"I'm going to go play with my friends," she said, getting up from the steps.

"What? No hug for your Uncle Gunner?" he said, his skinny arms opened wide.

"Meet you after school," she said to me, and made her escape without hugging Gunner. I wished I could go with her.

Gunner gave me a shove when he and my sister stepped up beside me. "Hey, I'm just kidding about the dork patrol stuff, pal. Lighten up. Hey," he said, turning back to Ronie, "do you think I could borrow a couple bucks? I have a feeling it's going to be a good day. I'll totally pay you back, but I need to get a drink to wet the instrument." He lifted his chin and rubbed his neck.

"It's going to be a good day?" I asked. "What's a good day for a guy who sits on the couch all day playing video games?"

"Songwriting," he snapped. "All the best musicians write their own stuff, you little brat."

I rolled my eyes. The guy was so disgustingly self-important. Combine that with the fact that Ronie pretty much gave Gunner all the money she made from coaching gymnastics and the dude was just unbearable. She never said anything about the money, but I knew it bothered her. Training with Maxim Gorelov was her dream so every time he took her cash she got grumpy and eventually that grumpiness spilled over onto me. Plus, I was pretty sure Gunner took money out of Ronie's wallet whenever he wanted. It wasn't like Ronie and I were ever BFFs but we didn't fight nearly as much before the wannabe came along.

"Besides," he continued, lowering his face so he was eye-to-eye with me, "playing video games is part of my *process*."

Marcus laughed, and Gunner turned toward him.

Ronie fished out a few bills from her purse and gave them to Gunner. He pulled her close and kissed her before taking off on his bike.

"Why do you put up with him?" I asked.

She gave me a narrow-eyed look and walked away without a word.

"You know," Marcus said, "if we're going to do this whole Revenger thing we're going to need to build up a reputation. I'm thinking we'll need some kind of portfolio where people can see what we've done, which means we're going to need to hit a few quick targets *pro bono*."

I knew exactly what he was thinking and stared down the street at Gunner as he rode away on his bike. "You're absolutely right," I said. "And you know, I think Gunner is just begging to be our first target. It'd be good for us, Ronie, and the public in general."

Marcus smiled. "It would be a public service. I mean, people should thank us for keeping the guy's music out of the airwaves. I wouldn't be surprised if we got the key to the city."

"It's settled, then," I said. "Gunner's days as a wannabe rock star are officially numbered."

CHAPTER 3

As we stepped into the classroom, Marcus said, "Do you want people to know it's us, or should we be anonymous? And—"

"Anonymous about what? What are you guys talking about?"

We turned to see Janet Everton's face inches from ours. Janet was the class gossip. She knew everything about everyone, not just in our class but the whole school. She even had dirt on most of the teachers and some of the kids' parents.

"We were talking about sending you a love letter, Janet." Marcus made a goofy face and batted his eyes at her. "We couldn't decide if it should be from a secret admirer or if we should just put it out there how much we both love you."

"Secret," she said quickly. "That way I can imagine it came from someone who is actually intelligent and handsome, and I won't vomit on my new shoes."

I pulled Marcus to our desks at the back of the class and whispered, "Anonymous. We have got to be anonymous. She'll tell the world if she finds out what we're up to. Our plans would be over. No one's gonna hire us if they know we're kids."

He nodded, studying Janet from across the room. "Is it just me or does she remind you of a dolphin?"

"Dolphin? What the heck does a—" I grabbed him by his shoulders and shook him. "You heard me, right?"

"Yeah, yeah, I heard." He pushed my hands away. "Don't worry. This'll be fun. I'll make the website tonight."

"Website?"

"Would you rather just leave leaflets on people's cars with your parents' phone numbers? Something like: 'Revenger for hire. Call my mom for a free consultation. Leave a message if you call after my bedtime.'"

"Make the site," I grumbled.

"Consider it done... Revenger."

During the rest of the day Marcus and I used every ounce of free time batting around ideas for the business and coming up with strategies for handling the types of requests we might get. But more than anything we worked on how we'd get rid of Gunner.

"It has to be something that sticks," I said. "Something that keeps him away from my sister long enough for her to realize she's better without him."

"We could get him locked up," Marcus said. "Plant some drugs on the guy and call the cops."

"Yeah, but this isn't about totally destroying him," I said. "I don't want the guy to go to prison. I just want him out of Ronie's life because that's the only way he'll be out of mine. Besides, we don't even know where to buy drugs. Even if we did I don't really feel like doing high school in juvenile detention after we got ourselves busted, which we totally would."

Marcus tapped his chin. "A stint in juvie would do wonders for building street cred. But I see your point. You're the idea guy, so what do you have in mind?"

I had several ideas, but none that I thought would really work. I imagined how perfect it would be if the jerk just went away to college, like in another state. Or another country. Marcus used our computer science period to hack Gunner's grades. His C-minus average might have gotten him into the local community college if he had a knock-your-socks-off essay to help him, but no way was Gunner Harvard material. We needed to keep thinking.

"Why does Gunner have to be so annoying," Sky asked when we met her after school.

"It's possible he has a non-life-threatening brain tumor that makes him stupid," I said. "Thanks a lot for bailing on us. I had to listen to your 'Uncle Gunner' talk about how playing video games is part of his process."

"Basically the usual torment," Marcus said.

"He's gross," Sky said. "Can I go play with my friends before we go home?"

"Sure," I said.

Marcus and I went to the tetherball pole while Sky played on the swings. Marcus smacked the ball back to me. It wound up on its rope and I smacked it back to unwind it. I pictured Gunner's face on the ball.

"What about running over his guitar?" Marcus asked.

"Not going to get rid of him," I said. "Besides, he plays bongos too. You do not want him switching back to bongos. The guy even makes *them* go out of tune. Plus it wouldn't stop the singing."

Marcus caught the tetherball. "How about something that would make Ronie hate him?"

I thought about all the disgusting things Gunner already did. He belched, scratched his butt in public, treated any kid as an audience waiting to love his latest song, and never took Ronie anywhere unless she paid for it. "I think Gunner's already covered those bases. We need something that will make him go away. Far, far away."

"Like another galaxy? Rocket packs?"

"Who's getting rocket packs?" It was Janet again. I turned around slowly. She stood there, fists on hips, just staring at us.

"Do you realize how creepy it is that you're just always around?" I asked.

"I know you two are up to something."

"You caught us," Marcus said. "We were planning a surprise party for you. I wanted to get you a set of rocket packs. You know"—he pointed to the sky—"so you could finally go back to your home planet."

"You're hysterical."

“Sky!” I called across the grounds. “Let’s go.”

“I’ll figure it out, you know,” Janet said. “I always figure stuff out.”

It was time for Janet to go, and Marcus clearly had the same thought because he suddenly yelled, “What was that, Janet? You want to make out with me? Right here?”

There weren’t a lot of people on the field, but those who were turned and stared and most of them started laughing. Janet turned pink and stomped away.

“When we finish with Gunner, I say we consider adding her to the list,” Marcus said.

“We’ll talk about it,” I said. But the truth was, Janet usually *did* figure stuff out. She was actually really smart (don’t ever tell her I said so), but she was also a total gossip queen. We’d need to keep an eye on her. She had the potential to ruin everything.

CHAPTER 4

On Saturday morning I woke up to my computer beeping that I had a message. It was from Marcus: GET OVER TO MY PLACE ASAP. Capital letters usually meant Marcus was panicking about something.

I almost called him, but it was just after six in the morning and since neither one of us had cell phones yet I'd have had to call his house. His parents were cool but not wake-us-up-at-six-in-the-morning cool. I messaged him back that I was on my way.

It was six-thirty by the time I showered, got dressed, and scarfed down a bowl of cereal. I jotted a quick note to my parents so they'd know where I'd gone and threw my bag over my shoulder. I checked my computer one more time before I left, and Marcus had already replied half a dozen times telling me to hurry up, in increasingly larger font. He'd even written his last message in red with a panic-faced emoticon.

Marcus didn't live far. It wasn't even seven when I got there, but his door was wide open and he was pacing in and out of the front door.

"C'mon," he said as I dropped my bike on his lawn and followed him inside.

"What's going on?" I asked.

He had a huge grin on his face and prodded me down the hall and into his room, where his cat, Penny, sat at his desk chair. He'd had Penny since she was a kitten and he was a baby and she often sat next to him while he worked.

Marcus wasn't your average computer nerd. He was pretty good at sports and liked biking and skateboarding but he was a total tech-head and his parents were too. Marcus had the latest of everything computer related. Quad-processor, speed-of-light stuff. Walking into his room was like walking onto the bridge of a starship: cool everywhere you looked.

He picked Penny up from his chair and sat down. She immediately hopped back up on his lap as he waved his hands toward the monitors like a magician. He flicked on the screen to reveal the homepage for THE REVENGERS.

"You already built it?" I asked, leaning forward.

"Of course I did."

It looked pretty incredible. His parents were web marketers and computer programmers and had taught Marcus how to build really cool websites. He'd been at it since he was old enough to turn on a computer and had dozens of sites. There was givememoney.com and freemarcus.com, which were both basically places where people could donate money to help free Marcus from the horrors of living in the middle class. He was honest about it. He thought people would give money because they thought it was funny.

No one ever did.

He did have one website that made money, and it was my favorite: shirtlesspicturesofjohnnyswag.com. It was exactly what it sounded like. For a dollar a year, you could get every picture that popped up online with pop star Johnny Swag shirtless. Disturbingly genius.

Marcus had over a hundred subscribers last time he checked. They were called Swagettes, and were mostly young girls with a few moms and guys thrown in. Marcus was making a hundred bucks a year for doing almost nothing.

There was nothing funny about the Revengers website though. It opened on an image of a guy backlit so you couldn't see his face. Beneath him a caption read: *Revengers*. A message box gave instructions:

We are the Revengers. We handle problems no one else will and we handle them like bosses. You need someone to leave you alone? Have a brother who won't stop giving you atomic wedgies? A bully who needs to learn a lesson? An angry neighbor who won't let you cut across their lawn to get home? Tell us about it. If we're interested, we'll solve your problem Revenger-style. When that happens, use the tip button. Seriously! Tip us or you might be the next one targeted by THE REVENGERS!

"Very cool!" I said.

"They just click the DONATE NOW button when they want to pay us for our services. I have a numbered payment account that no one can trace back to us. Just like a spy account—for our spy camp."

"It's awesome, Marcus. You did good. But it's not exactly worthy of how panicked you were. Why didn't you just send me a link? Why'd you want me over here so early?"

Marcus smiled. "I'm not excited about the website. That part was easy. I'm excited because I made the site live last night and I received an email less than an hour later."

"What do you mean? We got someone wanting to hire us? How'd they find out about us so fast?"

"My Google algorithms are advanced, bro. I've got 'em limited to a fifteen-mile radius. Check this out." He opened his email and this cat face lunged out of the screen at us.

"Whoa!" I jumped back. Even Penny scrambled our of Marcus's lap. "Those fangs are like a mile long."

The subject line read: EVIL CAT

Marcus scrolled down from the photo to the text: PLEASE HELP US. A STRAY IS TERRORIZING OUR NEIGHBORHOOD. EVIL KITTY WILL KILL ANYTHING THAT COMES NEAR. YOU PROBABLY THINK I'M CRAZY, BUT I'M NOT. PLEASE, JUST WATCH THIS!

Clicking on the video link, Marcus pulled up a shaky image of a street lined with houses. "Isn't that Oak Street?" I asked.

"Yeah, looks like it. That's only a couple miles away. But just wait until you see this."

"Oh... wow!"

The *wow* practically fell out of my mouth as a dog-sized cat leaped out at a kid on a bike. The cat swiped at the bike tires, instantly flattening one. The kid toppled over, got up, and ran. A mailman came into the picture. He saw the cat and stopped.

The cat saw him and charged. Mail flew into the air. The cat headed straight for the mailman's leg. Orange fur flew. We didn't have sound, but the mailman's mouth opened with a scream. He started kicking but the cat had his leg. He swung his bag and knocked the cat off him. The guy ran, his shredded pants leg flapping. The cat shook himself off then started prowling straight toward the camera.

Shaky-cam went ultra shaky. The cat lunged and everything froze with giant white fangs headed for the camera.

Marcus swiveled his chair so he could face me. "Look, I know Gunner is a problem for you, and I'm fully on board with getting that guy out of the picture. But dude, if the Revengers take care of this cat, our reputation will explode."

"Yeah, Gunner'll have to wait. Let's go check out this killer cat."

We grabbed our bikes and headed for Oak Street.

CHAPTER 5

Oak Street was a narrow street lined with elm trees. They'd been oak trees at one time, but some tree sickness killed every last one of them. The town replanted elms instead since the local nursery was having a sale. Giant gnarled trunks and limbs rose up on either side of the street and tangled overhead to block the sky. I thought about how lions liked to hang out in trees. At least that's what National Geographic had shown in one of their specials.

We rode down the street, the squeak of rusting bike chains the only sound. No bird calls. No dogs barking. No kids yelling and laughing while playing football in the street. It was still kind of early, but the utter silence made the street feel eerie.

We pulled over when we spotted the big white house from the cat video, hopping off our bikes.

Marcus looked around. "Do you—?"

"Shhhh," I said. "Hear that?" Leaves rustled overhead but there was no wind. I looked up.

Big yellow eyes stared down at me. The cat was crouching in a way that told us he was ready to pounce at any moment..

"Back up. Slowly," I told Marcus, moving very carefully out of the cat's jumping range. The goal was to be smooth, but Marcus leapt on his bike, startling the cat, who jumped down off his branch headed straight toward us. Marcus ducked, and the cat missed his head by an inch. With a yell, we rode. But Evil Cat wasn't done with us.

I pedaled as hard and as fast as I could but he was right there at my ankles.

"Faster!" I yelled.

I wasn't fast enough. He dug his claws into my jeans, ripping them straight through. Somehow I was able to shake off the bristling ball of orange fur. We pedaled even harder, finally putting some distance between us and the cat. Just when I started to relax I heard him growl and hiss and yowl. I glanced back to see him charging after us. *You have to be kidding me!*

"Head for the main street!" I yelled.

Like a tiger chasing an antelope, the cat tore across lawns and over fences trying to cut us off. He raced along the top of a fence right beside us, and launched himself at me just as I turned my bike around a corner. I lowered my head and felt Evil Cat bounce off my helmet. Marcus let out a piercing scream that might have made me laugh if I hadn't been racing for my life.

We pedaled as hard as we could. I kept my focus forward and my head down as I picked up speed. My heart pounded like it wanted out of my chest as much as I wanted out of that neighborhood. Rounding a corner, we hit the main street. I slowed down and glanced back. Marcus turned the corner and pulled up next to me. The cat was gone.

"Did we... did it... was that...?"

I glanced down at my ankle. Pulling up my torn jeans I

showed Marcus the scratch. "Yeah, Evil Cat strikes again. I need a drink."

We found a store that sold sodas and parked our bikes out front. We plopped onto the curb and I waited until my hands stopped shaking, hoping that my voice didn't tremble when I spoke. "You think he has an owner?"

"Are you kidding me?" Marcus said. "That raggedy mean thing? The only owner he might have is Lucifer."

"True," I said. Still, we needed to catch him, get him off the streets. "Think we could catch it in a sack? Let it loose at the city dump or someplace where it'll be someone else's problem?"

"You really want to try and put that tornado in a bag?"

I shrugged. "It could work."

"Okay. Where do we get a strong enough bag?"

It took a couple days, but eventually we found what we needed at Anderson's Feed and Tack. They had these heavy paper bags that hold like fifty pounds of food for horses and cows. We found some empty ones in a dumpster out back and asked the guy in the store if we could take them.

"Sure," he said, chewing on a toothpick.

"Let me ask you a question," Marcus said. "How strong are these things? Like, say—could a cat claw his way out of it?"

The guy narrowed his eyes at Marcus. "Now why would a cat even *be* in the bag in the first place? What are you boys up to?"

"Er, nothing," I said. "Just a science project thing."

"Huh," he said, totally not believing us. "Well, take what

you want but remember—we're animal lovers around here."

As we left, I said, "I don't think Evil Cat technically qualifies as an animal."

At home we grabbed a few lengths of heavy twine to go with our heavy bags. Then, despite the fact that it was early fall and still pretty warm, we dressed in winter clothes and headed back to the cat's lair.

"Okay," Marcus said. "Let's go over the plan one more time."

"We'll go into the neighborhood on foot. Since you're the bait, you'll get it to run after you toward me. I'll be hiding behind that big bush next to the white house and grab it as it runs after you."

"Why do I have to be the bait?"

"You want to be the one to grab him?" I held out the bag. "Be my guest. The one with the bag is the only one who has to actually touch the beast."

Marcus glanced at the bag. The paper was thick but not as thick as a cat's claws... especially Evil Cat's claws, which I knew from personal experience were more like razors. "Fine, I'll give being the bait a try."

"Yeah, I figured. Now where is that beast?"

We looked around but didn't see any trace of Evil Cat. No screams of panic from the neighbors, either.

"Let's get into position so we're ready for him," I said.

We set out the bowl of milk we hoped he'd be interested

in drinking.

"Maybe he'd prefer the heart of a buffalo," Marcus said.

Once the milk was set and we were in our hiding places, we sat and waited. And waited. We had to wait for almost an hour before he finally showed up again. Evil Cat walked down the sidewalk, his long orange tail flicking back and forth like he owned the street. Which he totally did.

I nodded to Marcus and he stepped out from the hiding spot.

"Here, kitty kitty." He patted his thigh and spoke in one of those high-pitched voices people are always talking to babies with. "C'mon, pretty kitty. Come and get me, you crazy-psycho-monster-kitty."

Evil Cat's ears flattened and his eyes narrowed.

"I wouldn't overdo it if I were you," I whispered.

Marcus waved at him and blew it a kiss. "If I'm going to be attacked by this monster, I'll feel better if I kind of deserve it."

The cat put his head down and started toward Marcus like a lion in the jungle.

"Sweet, pretty kitty. Come here you darling little... oh, no..."

The cat dipped his long body low to the ground and started past the bowl of milk and straight toward Marcus, who fell back a step.

"Just wait a second," I whispered to him. "Not yet."

The cat moved slowly, his belly skimming the ground as he crept closer. Marcus took two more steps back until he was nearly in the street. “He’s coming for me, not the milk,” he squeaked.

“You’ll be fine,” I told him, although remembering how the cat had torn apart that kid’s bike tire had me questioning our plan.

The cat bounded forward so fast I almost missed him.

Almost.

I lunged out with the bag held open. The cat’s eyes were locked on Marcus, his claws reaching out for him. I got most of his head into the bag but his back claws were thrashing everywhere.

“Help!” I yelled. Marcus tackled the bag and pushed the cat’s fuzzy butt inside. Claws pierced through the paper. “This isn’t going to hold!” I wrapped the twine around the top of the bag and Marcus whipped off his jacket and wrapped it around the bag. Low, angry growls rose up from inside. I sat back on my heels. Cat scratches crisscrossed my skin like I’d just run through a cactus forest. Only then did I feel the sting of it. My adrenaline was pumping so hard I hadn’t noticed the pain.

"Okay, where to now?" Marcus asked.

Because the cat was thrashing around inside we had to take turns carrying the cat and pushing the bikes. As we transported Evil Cat to his new home far, far away from Oak Street and the innocent children—and bikes—of the neighborhood, we felt the beast calm down enough that we could ride our bikes again. We rode as hard as we could and must've gone ten miles, taking turns carrying the bag. We got to the edge of town, to an open area that was going to be a new shopping center. The cleared land backed onto a forest and I imagined there'd be plenty of mice for the cat to eat... or elk and deer, since that's probably what it preferred.

"Get ready to run," I told Marcus.

He was already on his bike, holding mine for me. I pulled in a breath, carefully untied the twine from the bag and then heaved the whole thing away from me. I ran for my bike and jumped on. We pedaled like crazy, hearing thrashing behind us. I glanced back in time to see the cat launch through the bag's opening and spin around in a circle. It spotted a few crows pecking at the ground a short distance away. It shot like a bolt of orange lightning toward the birds—there was a lot of screeching and feathers. I pedaled harder to put more distance between us and Evil Cat. I didn't look behind us again until we were in a neighborhood miles away and I could hear birds chirping happily again.

Letting out a breath, I turned to Marcus and we swapped

high-fives.

The rest of the weekend was spent with a bottle of iodine and a box of Band-Aids. Monday after school, Ronie walked Sky home while Marcus and I rode back to the see the mailman make his route and watch the kids on Oak Street enjoy their new freedom. "It's going to be a celebration," Marcus said, smiling. "People will be walking their dogs, kids will be tossing balls on their lawns, and bikes can once again ride—" Marcus broke off and skidded to a halt.

I pulled up next to him. "What?"

He pointed to one of the elm trees.

There on the empty street, perched on a thick branch, a familiar orange ball loomed. "No. It's got to be a different cat. Or a..."

The cat turned its head. Yellow eyes stared at us, narrowed and glinting with evil while his tail slowly swatted back and forth. No mistaking that splash of white over one eye or that huge body.

Evil Cat was back.

CHAPTER 6

"Please tell me we don't have to go through nine lives to get that cat?" Marcus said once we'd pedaled away from Evil Cat and back to the safety of our neighborhood. It was time to regroup. Again.

"Maybe he's got a twin."

"Good twin to go with the evil one?" Marcus said. "Maybe we should have stuck around to see if the new one wanted to cuddle."

I didn't believe it either. "You ever seen anything like this with Penny?"

"No way," Marcus said. "My cat only gets upset if I don't feed her by seven a.m. And then she only walks on my head in bed. Usually I just cuddle with her until I'm ready to get up. I swear she'd rather have love than food."

"I'm going to search the net for info on cats," I said. "Maybe there's a tutorial somewhere about training them or something."

"Try searching for lion taming," Marcus suggested as we pulled into his driveway. "That might give us some better ideas to work with." He leaned his bike against his garage and headed toward his front door. "Better yet," he called back, "you should see if you can find a priest or something, because I think that cat might just be flat-out evil. For all we know he's possessed and needs a bath in holy water to drive the demons out of him."

That was a pretty good suggestion and I laughed about it on the way home. But I was starting to feel frustrated. This was supposed to be a simple assignment for us—for the Revengers—and if we couldn't handle a cat, how were we going to handle people with really important problems?

That night I learned the hard way that the last thing you want to search for online is cats. I'm not sure who invented the Internet, but it's cat people who run it now. There are more search results for cats than any other topic on the planet. It's as if cat people think every single thing their balls of fur do is worthy of uploading online. It's a virtual cat minefield.

I found lots of stuff about feeding cats and cat care and training cats to do dumb tricks. My eyes were crossed from watching too many videos, but I hadn't found one word on how to turn an angry cat into a nice one. The last video I saw gave me an idea, though. It showed a cat, next to a street musician, pawing at the guy's guitar while it sat in the open case. I sent Marcus a link and called him.

"Did you get it?"

"What?"

"The link. Did you—?"

"Oh that. You want to teach Evil Cat how to play guitar, or did you want to get the cat on YouTube? Or... oh, hey, you want to stuff the cat in Gunner's guitar case? Maybe see if his music would make the cat run away? Worst thing that could happen is he attacks Gunner. That wouldn't be a bad thing, right? Does Gunner even have a case for his guitar?"

"The only way he has a case is if Ronie bought it for him—but that's not important. Did you look at the number of hits on that video? It reminded me of the one thing Ronie worries about with Gunner, and that's that he'll become a busker."

"Busker? You mean those guys who clean tables in restaurants? I don't think she has to worry about that. The guy's way too lazy to get a job."

"Not *busser. Busker.* As in street performers. Ronie hates those guys and will totally take the long way around to avoid 'em. I heard her tell one guy that if he valued his art he should practice and try out for *Pop Star Nation*. You should see her face whenever someone suggests Gunner perform downtown. If the guy wasn't so lazy he'd probably do it."

"So if she sees Gunner playing on the street it's the end of him?"

I shook my head. "Think bigger. We need to make it so *everyone* sees him. All her friends, people she does gymnastics with, even strangers who might run into them when they're out."

"I get it. We need to put him somewhere everyone'll see him."

"Exactly. Okay, first things first. I need some links to show Gunner, links that will convince him the best—the easiest—path to success is to take his screech-fest to the streets. Then we follow him, record it, put it online, and send links to everyone. Make sure all of Ronie's friends see."

"Leave it to me," Marcus said. "I know exactly what we need. But what about Evil Cat?"

"We need a plan for that monster too. But let's shift our focus to Gunner for now. If we can show that the Revengers can take care of anything—human or beast—we'll have more business than we can handle."

"And more money for the spy camp pot," Marcus said.

"Yep, that too."

Marcus more than came through for me. The next day after school he showed me the videos he'd grabbed. He'd even found guys who looked a lot like Gunner with curly hair and sagging jeans. Of course, these guys actually seemed capable of playing their guitars but I didn't think Gunner would notice that part.

"I still don't get how you're going to convince Gunner to copy these guys."

I smiled. "Revengers always have a plan."

"Do we?" Marcus asked.

"Yes."

"Really? 'Cause I thought we were kind of flying by the seats of our pants."

"We're not," I said. "We have a plan."

He rolled his eyes. "I'll go ahead and take your word for that."

CHAPTER 7

I did have a plan, and it went into action the next day. After school I rushed home with Sky to get ready.

"Let's have a race," I told her. "Whoever gets home first gets the TV."

She shot off like a cannon down the sidewalk. I followed close behind. She could have the TV—I had Revengers work to do.

Gunner always came over after Ronie got home from school, before she went to gymnastics and before our parents got home from work. I think he knew my dad didn't like him, which meant he had at least one functioning brain cell.

Ronie was home but up in her room, which was good since I wanted to catch Gunner before she saw him. I took Ronie's laptop off the kitchen table and snuck it out to the steps on the front porch. I had a huge bag of Doritos with me—which I was pretty sure was perfect lazy-wannabe-rock-star bait. Just like the milk with Evil Cat, I was going to bait Gunner with powder cheesy goodness.

I heard Gunner's car choking down the street a mile off,

which also meant Ronie could probably hear him from up in her room. I had to be fast.

Gunner's rusted old Honda backfired when he pulled up to our curb and lurched forward once before it sputtered to a stop. I ripped open the Doritos and started the videos.

Gunner stepped out of his car and stood back examining the heap like it was the world's coolest sports car. Then he turned and headed toward me. I gave him a wave.

"Hey, Gunner. Want some Doritos?" It was like asking a shark if it wanted a bite of a seal. Gunner never turned down free food.

He strolled over. He had his guitar slung over his back and he gave me a wary glance but grabbed the whole bag and started attacking them. He crammed handfuls into his gob. I may be a guy, and a kid, but it was pretty gross.

"Thanks, little man," he said. He ruffled my hair with his cheesy Dorito hand, getting unpronounceable ingredients in my hair. Then he took the same hand and jammed it back in the bag. Chomping on another chip, he said, "This is just what I need after a long day of songwriting."

I dusted the chip dust out of my hair and imagined him getting eaten by Evil Cat and managed to smile. "Have you seen these videos? They've gotten, like, mega hits." I grabbed the Doritos back and moved them to the side so Gunner had to lean across the videos to get to the chips. "You ever thought about playing on the street like this? Seems like a great way to get your music out there. I mean, look at the views on these videos! And you know, I heard guys like Bob Dylan got their start playing on the street."

"Who?"

"Uh... never mind. Will you look at that? Over a hundred thousand views for this guy. Bet he's got a record contract already."

"I've thought about the street-playing thing but it's a tough slog to play out there. Sitting in the heat or rain or cold, people tossing change at you, not getting that audience feedback like you would on a stage in a club. You know—that energy? Not to mention it would cut into my songwriting time."

"Uh-huh, I'm sure it would be hard to manage with your busy schedule." I tried hard to sound sincere but he gave me a look like he could hear sarcasm in my voice. I had to recover. "But I'm telling you, these guys all got mega-million-dollar contracts just for playing a few songs in the streets. Plus it's a great way to test-run your music. You can ask people what they think of your stuff. You can't do that in a club. You gotta be polished. I'm telling you, this way is practically guaranteed."

He chomped another chip. "Guaranteed, eh?"

I could feel him coming around. "Check out this guy," I said. "He even kind of looks like you and he has like two million views on his videos. *Two million*."

Under his curly mop, Gunner's eyes lit up. "Two million?"

"Bet you could do better. Bet if you got a great spot, like

maybe near the mall, right when it gets busy, you'd have people lining up to hear you." I made a show of checking my watch. "It's probably pretty busy right now."

He nodded. "You've got a point, little man. I bet if I set up in the outdoor part of the mall by the food court, people would give me money just for making their meals more enjoyable."

"The smell of hot dogs and fries and the sound of your guitar?" I tilted my head. "It would be a brilliant combination." *A combination to create a group barf-fest*, I wanted to add.

Gunner grinned at me. "Little man, you're not as big a dork as I thought you were. That's not a bad idea."

I tried not to cringe at "little man" again, and instead focused on the plan. "Yeah, thanks. But like I said, it'll probably only work if you go fast. Like right now. No time like the present and all that stuff. Gotta get those good spots, right?"

He glanced at the house. I knew he was thinking about Ronie. Or maybe about the food in our kitchen. I shook the Doritos bag at him. "Here. Take this. I'll let Ronie know you're taking your music to the next level and that she should come by and hear you play."

He reached out to ruffle my hair. I ducked the move and pushed the Doritos bag into his hands. I didn't wait for any thanks or one more time of him calling me "little" anything. Waving him off, I ducked into the house just as his car coughed to a start and sputtered away. I closed Ronie's laptop and strolled into the kitchen, whistling.

Ronie came downstairs a minute later in her gymnastics gear and looked around. "Isn't Gunner here? He was going to hang out before I go to the gym. I told him I have a class at six."

Sky was chomping down a bowl of cereal and looked up and nodded, but she had a full mouth so she couldn't speak.

It was news I wanted to deliver to Ronie anyway, so I cleared my throat. "He was, but he said it's time he took his music seriously and he left."

"Left? Left where?" Ronie opened the front door and looked outside.

I smiled. "He said something about trying out the whole busker scene. He's going to the mall to put on a little impromptu concert."

Ronie's face dropped and a gasp slipped past her lips. "What do you mean?"

"He's under the impression that a record deal is in the cards," I said. "He's sure a mall performance is exactly what he needs." I held up my finger. "Wait, don't your friends usually hang out at the mall after school? I wonder if they'll see him perform."

"You better not be messing with me, Jared," she snapped. "Because if you're lying I'll tell all your friends I caught you trying on one of my bras."

I coughed.

"You wouldn't dare," I said.

The smirk on her face told me she totally would. I took a

second and wondered if my plan could backfire. No, I'd thought it through. Gunner would never give me credit for his master plan. I grabbed a carton of chocolate milk out of the fridge. "Guess you'll have to go to the mall to see if I'm lying or not."

She grabbed the keys to the car. Then she grabbed Sky and then she grabbed me. "You're coming."

CHAPTER 8

On any other day I'd rather eat cockroaches than go to the mall with Ronie, but this was going to be great. I had to see it. So I didn't actually try to fight it. Marcus had headed there right after school, so he would beat Gunner for sure.

We walked down the sidewalks of the outdoor part of the mall, the sun shining down on a perfect day. Perfect for the blowup that was about to happen, that is.

Sky was skipping along beside me but suddenly stopped, her nose wrinkled. "Is there a pet store around here?"

"No," I said. "Why?"

"Because it sounds like a cat is moaning somewhere. Or maybe being tortured."

As soon as she said it, I heard it. But it wasn't an animal being tortured—it was Gunner, "singing."

We were near the food court and although we couldn't actually see him, I knew that no one else could make a guitar sound like a screaming animal. I had to give it to Gunner: he couldn't sing, but he belted out every word like he believed he could.

I caught sight of Marcus near the taco place. He had an

unobstructed line of sight to Gunner's performance and his dad's camera in his hands. I smiled when I spotted Ronie's best friends, Becky and Charity, by the ice cream place, trying (unsuccessfully) not to laugh. They saw Ronie and rushed over just as Gunner launched into his next song.

"Ronie, you should have told us," Becky said.

"He gave this great talk about how art needs to be for everyone and how music has to be free or it's just a commercial sell-out." Charity giggled again.

Ronie was paralyzed. She stood stock still, staring at Gunner with wide, unbelieving eyes.

"He's incredible," Becky said.

I couldn't believe what they were saying. No way could they be enjoying this garbage. They focused their attention back to Gunner and their eyes went all glossy. A small crowd had gathered around Gunner and one of the kids was recording his performance on her cell phone. Gunner threw his head back, tossing his curls.

Ain' t no girl
In this world
Gonna love me
Like you, Pearl

"Who's Pearl?" Sky asked.

Charity giggled again and Becky sighed. "He's amazing. I saw a guy drop ten dollars in the coat he put out on the floor.

So cool he put out a leather jacket like that."

Ronie straightened. She smiled at her friends. "Yeah, Gunner's an original."

I heard a groan. It was mine.

"Why do you look so miserable? This guy is incredible!"

I turned to see Janet standing behind me. I let out another groan. "What are you doing here?"

"I was buying socks to match my new belt, but then I heard the sweetest, most passionate sound on earth and had to come find out what it was. And that's when I saw him." Her eyes gleamed adoration as she looked toward Gunner. I wanted to vomit right then and there.

"You think Gunner is good?" I asked.

She turned to look at me. "You *know* him?"

Before I could I could explain the level of douchebaggery that is Gunner to Janet, Ronie punched my arm. She took Sky's hand but kept her eyes on Gunner. "Let's go sit and listen to Gunner before I have to go to work. We'll get ice cream."

I glanced across the mall to where Marcus stood. He put out his hands to the side in a "what gives?" gesture. I gave him a shrug and followed Ronie, away from Janet.

A few days later I met up with Marcus before school. He ran his fingers through his hair when he saw me. "We've created a monster."

"No kidding," I said. "The guy's doing street performances all over town. He's outside of coffee shops and cafes, right in the center of town even."

"At least you don't have to see him as much, right?"

I shook my head. "He only does it during the day. He's at my house all the time, only now he's cockier than ever." I blew out a breath. "Did you put his video online?"

"I was going to," Marcus said, "but someone from the mall beat me to it. It's like that guy on *Pop Star Nation*—remember? That guy who was so bad but everyone voted for him as a joke? Anyway, I figured it was better if we just used the video someone else uploaded since it keeps us unconnected from the next phase of our plan."

"Good thinking," I said.

"How's Ronie taking it?" Marcus asked.

"Great. Which sucks. She doesn't even hate buskers anymore. She spent a half hour telling me how anyone who plays on the street is dedicated to their craft."

Marcus stuck a finger down his throat and made gagging sounds.

"Tell me about it." I hefted my backpack up on my shoulder.

"I've got even more bad news for you. Evil Cat struck again. We got another email from the Oak Street kids begging us to help. They promised us a big tip if the Revengers will take out that cat. They said the whole street is unsafe. I said we'd take care of it."

I nodded. "How much time do we need for the next phase of our plan with Gunner?"

"I'll need a day or two to create the bot."

"Fine," I said. "Since our get-rid-of-Gunner plan isn't going quite so well, let's go back to the cat. And this time I know just where to take him."

CHAPTER 9

School seemed to go on forever the way it does when you have something else you want to do instead. But as much as I wanted to get out and do some good—or some bad, depending on your point of view—I wasn't looking forward to facing off with Evil Cat. The last scratches had just started to heal. Even if things went well, I knew I'd end up with more marks. If our reputation wasn't on the line I'd never have set foot on that street again.

This time, however, instead of a bag to hold the beast in, we got a box. A big one. My neighbor had just gotten a new baby car seat and it came in this giant hunk of cardboard. I'd also borrowed Sky's little red wagon and put a rope on the handle. We took it all to Oak Street, where we set up the trap.

I had Marcus set out the box and prop one side up with a stick, attaching a string to the stick. I opened a can of tuna, waved it around a little to get the scent wafting through the air, then stuck it under the box. It was totally something you'd see in a cartoon, but we figured it was probably based on some kind of science.

We hid behind the bushes next to an elm tree. A half hour later the cat came strutting down the street, the big man on campus. Which he had proven over and over that he was.

Marcus started chanting "Eat it! Eat it! Eat it!" under his breath. I waited with my hands clenched into fists. Evil Cat sat down next to the box and began washing its paws. I put my face in my palm but Marcus nudged me with his elbow. "Look," he whispered.

The cat stopped washing. Slowly, it turned and sniffed the box. He slipped under. Marcus pulled the string. The box slammed down. Then it started bucking up and shooting across the pavement as Evil Cat went crazy inside. I ran over and threw myself on top of it.

"How do we get it closed?" Marcus asked.

Something we hadn't thought of. Great. The cat was freaking out inside the box, growling, moaning, basically telling us that we were going to pay for this once he got his claws on us. I couldn't let that happen. Somehow I managed to shout, "We need to find more cardboard!"

The cat thrashed around inside but I weighed more than he could lift so I managed to keep him inside. I stayed on the box while Marcus tore off, checking the neighbors' garbage cans for more cardboard. When he returned a couple of minutes later, the cat had calmed down—or at least he had stopped thrashing against the walls. Marcus slid the extra cardboard under the opening at the bottom. The box shook again and this time Evil

Cat actually got a couple of claws through the cardboard.

Marcus backed away a step. “That is one angry cat.”

“Yeah, so whatever we do, let’s not let him out.”

Low growls rumbled out of the box. I taped the whole thing together with some duct tape. Sitting back, I wiped the sweat from my eyes.

“Think it’ll hold?” Marcus asked.

“It better.” We hauled the box over to the wagon. I grabbed the rope and told Marcus to ride behind me. “If you see so much as a whisker sticking out, yell.”

“Oh, I’ll do better than that,” he said, “I’ll scream like a girl.”

He didn’t have to. We made it to First Valley Vet without any trouble at all. Marcus pulled up next to me on his bike.

"You don't think the vet's going to... you know... put him to sleep, do you?"

"I think vets tend to aim for helping animals before killing them. But why do you care? Have you grown attached to this monster? Did I miss the bonding time you had while he was chasing you down the street?"

"Nah, I was just going to ask if I could keep the head and mount it on my wall," he joked.

"Yeah right," I said. "Just try not to cry when the cat gets scared in there." Marcus loved his cat, Penny. Not that I hated animals—it was just that this thing was more of a beast than anything else.

"Maybe the vet will fix his problem and find him a good home," I said.

"Ah—fix. I get it." Marcus smirked. "Snip snip, and one more cat that gets fat and lazy. Or maybe we could train this thing and use it as a tool for our jobs—you know, like a mascot for the Revengers. We'd be feared."

I climbed off my bike. "We'd be dead, because that cat would kill us. This beast is lethal. The sooner we get rid of him the better. Now shut up and help me."

That cat had to be twenty pounds or more of pure fury. The growling started up as soon as we lifted the box. A few thumps from inside told us we still had our prisoner. We'd gotten to the vet right before they closed so no one else was in the waiting room. It smelled pretty bad—as if most of animals had used the tiled floor as a litterbox. I wondered they just sprayed the room with a hose at the end of each day. With the exception of a few drawings of dogs and cats that hung on the white walls, the rest of the office looked pretty basic. I told the lady behind the counter we wanted to see the vet and she had us step right into an exam room. Marcus helped me heave the box onto a metal table.

The vet came in and I smiled. "Hey, Dr. Smith."

We hadn't had a pet in a long time, but Dr. Smith had helped us with our dog, Ginger, when she'd gotten really old. In fact, he was the reason she'd gotten to be so old in the first place. He knew his animals. I just hoped he could help with cats that were clearly possessed.

I told him we'd caught a stray that had been roaming around attacking people. "He's really, *really* aggressive." The box thumped and rocked, proving my point.

"Quick question," Marcus said. "Is it possible for a cat to be psychotic?" The doctor smiled and Marcus said, "No, seriously. This cat nearly killed a mailman."

Dr. Smith frowned. He had on scrubs and he rubbed a hand down one pant leg. "That's not good. The little guy could be quite sick—and you say animal control couldn't catch it?"

We shook our heads. "I know you might think we're exaggerating," I started, "but he's *really* aggressive."

"Yes," the doctor said, "you mentioned that."

"And big, too," Marcus added. "Like really big. Like,

might-have-spent-some-time-in-the-sewer-eating-toxic-waste-and-became-a-mutant big."

"Riiiight," Dr. Smith said. "Big and aggressive. Thanks for the heads-up, guys. How about we take a look at the poor thing?"

I glanced at the shaking, thumping box. "I'm not sure that's a great idea."

"Poor fellow's probably scared, is all. We're waiting on a backorder of diffuser cartridges—which would help keep the little guy relaxed but I think the three of us can handle one little cat."

Marcus and I swapped looks and I saw the same fear in his eyes that I felt. The good doctor was totally underestimating this fur ball. More than that, even if he was right and the cat was scared, it wasn't the only one.

Dr. Smith glanced at the top of the box and figured out how to peel back the duct tape to open it. Marcus stepped back. I braced myself. Dr. Smith opened a flap. Nothing happened. The doc peered into the box. I leaned forward to do the same. I saw ears pined back, yellow eyes sharp as cut glass, and a bristling ball of orange fur. The cat had a splash of white on its face like someone had thrown a bottle of cream at it at one time.

"Well, hello there, fella. Look at you. Let's just see what we've got here." The doc reached a hand into the box.

Orange fur flew out.

Spitting, claws extended, the cat came out swinging at anything and everyone. Marcus yelped and jumped up on a chair. I put up my arms to keep my face from getting clawed. Pain ripped down my arm. Even Dr. Smith jumped back. The cat landed on the exam table. He hunched there for a second, flicking his tail, his ears flat. Dr. Smith grabbed a towel to throw over the cat, but the cat took off again. It hit a counter and sent jars of dressings and swabs flying. The cat slammed into a computer monitor. Dr. Smith grabbed for the monitor.

Leaping, the cat snagged one of the drawings on the wall. It was of a smiling dog clearly drawn by a child. In one swipe, the orange monster tore the head of the dog right out of the frame and sent the rest of the picture to the floor. More glass shattered. The receptionist cracked open the door.

"Is there—?" She didn't get any more words out. The cat headed for her and ran between her legs. He swiped at her as he raced past. She jumped with a yelp. We all ran after the orange streak. I pushed into the reception room just in time to see the cat claw his way up the magazine rack. Pages flew. Evil Cat jumped onto one of the couches and tore into it, shredding the covering. With a growl, the cat headed for a window. He threw himself at the blinds, tearing them down. The last I saw of him was the flip of a fuzzy orange tail as he disappeared. The blinds crashed to the floor and the window's screen flapped in the breeze. The cat had ripped through it. Or maybe just punched his way out.

I walked back into the exam room, dazed. The receptionist sat on the floor, dabbing some kind of disinfectant on her legs and hissing at every dab. Dr. Smith cradled his monitor, which was about the only thing unbroken in the room. Marcus slowly eased down from the chair. I glanced at the doc. I hoped I wouldn't have to pay for the damage. Dr. Smith let out a breath and put down the monitor. He reached up to scratch his head.

"That, if I am not mistaken, happens to be a very rare breed of cat. A Burmese mix, I believe. He likely has hyperesthesia syndrome which makes them very aggressive. He needs medication and a stress-free environment to manage. But... when I touched him, I'm pretty sure I felt a lump from where an RFID chip was implanted. If that's the case, he's no stray. That cat has an owner. And if we can find the owner, we might be able to help the cat get back on track."

Once we'd left the vet's office, Marcus said, "If the Revengers can't even take care of a cat, our reputation will be destroyed before we even start. I almost wish I hadn't agreed to take on this monster."

Things had just gotten personal between us and that cat. We'd created the Revengers with the goal of building a reputation of ruthlessly taking care of problems that people couldn't take care of themselves. We were dangerous. We were not to be messed with. We hadn't proved it to anyone yet, but Marcus and I were on the same page: Revengers don't quit when the going gets tough. They get tougher.

CHAPTER 10

The bag hadn't worked. The box had almost worked, but I had a feeling the cat was smarter than us, and we got mostly As and Bs. Luckily, I had another ace up my sleeve.

I borrowed Ace, the German shepherd from next door, and we tried to use him to hunt down the cat. I mean, cats—even big cats—are afraid of dogs, right? It's supposed to be the natural order of things. And I was pretty sure German shepherds were the kind of dogs the police used, so Ace should really be intimidating, right? Well, this cat didn't get that message.

The cat took one look at Ace and started stalking him. I imagined we could've brought an entire K9 squad from the police station and he would have tried to take them all on. This was like Puss-in-Boots on steroids and Red Bull.

Ace took one look at the cat, whimpered, tucked his tail, pulled away, and took off in the opposite direction from Oak Street. It was silly for us to bring a dog that clearly wasn't battle tested and I made a mental note that we should bring Ace to our next paintball exercise.

"Coward!" Marcus shouted as we sprinted after Ace. After he turned back into the safety of his own yard, Marcus said, "We need something more like a tank. Maybe tranquilizer darts? Like for an elephant?"

I snapped my fingers. "That's it!" I raided my mom's supply of calming teas. She keeps about five different kinds for what she calls her "hard days." Those are the days where she brews her tea, takes a chocolate bar, and locks herself in the bathroom and leaves melted candles on the edge of the tub. Dad says a guy should never ask a woman how she can hang out in a bathroom for three hours. So I don't.

While I brewed up a dozen bags of tea I sent Marcus out to buy a pound of hamburger. I tried to boil the tea right down so most of the water was gone and all that remained was whatever made you calm from drinking the tea. I checked online to see if the teas were safe for animals and apparently they were. A few people on pet message boards said the teas worked wonders on their aggressive cats.

We formed the hamburger into a large patty and put it in a Tupperware container then poured what was left of the tea over it. It was more like a calming gravy. It oozed. I stabbed the meat with a fork to get the tea-sludge into it, and that seemed to work. Then I covered it up and we rode back to Oak Street.

We took our time so the meat could really soak up the tea. We left the meat out in the street for the evil beast then took a spot a safe distance away to watch and wait.

"You sure this won't hurt him?" Marcus asked. "Did you see the label on the box? It said you should consult a doctor before you drink if you're under twelve, pregnant, or breastfeeding."

I told him about the message boards I'd looked up, and that seemed to calm him down a bit. "Would you stop with the worrying about this thing?" I bumped his arm. "It's tea. It'll be fine. When we take him back to the vet, I'll tell Dr. Smith what we did. I even have the labels in my bag to show him. Now stop being a baby. We're Revengers for Pete's sake."

We found a hiding spot near the big white house. The flowering bushes hid us pretty well but we could see the Tupperware clearly. I glanced at the meat we'd set out. So far only the flies seemed interested in it. It was a bit hard to see, but I could've sworn a few flies landed on the meat and then tried to fly away only to fall back to the ground. One fly landed on my arm and it actually seemed to stagger before falling to the ground. I had high hopes this tea would work.

Like before, the neighborhood was freakishly quiet. We watched one woman pull up in her driveway, dash to her front door, and quickly lock it behind her. We wondered how this poor neighborhood had survived.

We had some time to wait so we played a game like I Spy, only instead of stupid stuff like "something green" or "something fluffy" we had to find things that looked destroyed by an evil feline. It was pretty easy—trees clawed, flower beds dug up, even a lawn gnome torn apart were just a few pieces of evidence showcasing Evil Cat's destruction. We weren't worried about being spotted as the Revengers. We were kids, and if anyone asked, we'd say someone gave us twenty dollars to catch a cat.

I also kept an eye out for Janet. If she saw us here after seeing us at the vet, she might start putting it together. Our cover would be blown just as we were getting started.

Marcus gestured toward another damaged part of the street when I heard a noise. The cat jumped down from a tree two houses ahead. He stretched and yawned and shook his orange fur back into place. The bits of white on his face reflected the sunlight. He lifted his head and sniffed.

"That's right, kitty. Nice fresh meat waiting for you. Bloody, just the way you like it," I whispered.

The cat took his time strolling down the sidewalk. I thought I saw the flick of a curtain as someone looked out to see if the street was safe, and went back to hiding when they glimpsed the cat.

Coming closer, the cat stopped and sniffed again. He caught sight of the meat and slowly headed that way. "That's it, monster-cat."

He sniffed at the air, several feet from the meat. Finally he lowered his body to the ground and, like a snake, practically slithered to the meat, sniffing it some more.

"What is he, some kind of drug-sniffing cat?" Marcus said.

"No. Look." The cat nibbled a small bite, tasting. Then he chomped down huge hunks of meat like he hadn't eaten in weeks. In seconds the hamburger vanished. He didn't stop until he'd lapped up all the tea in the dish. For good measure, he attacked the Tupperware with his mouth, gave his head a shake and tossed the plastic dish into the road.

We waited. The cat sat back on his haunches to wash his paws. This time I'd come prepared. Dr. Smith had a towel ready for the cat when he had gone crazy in his office, and I'd done one better. I'd brought a heavy-duty army blanket from the emergency supplies in our garage. The cat finally yawned. I motioned for Marcus to grab one side of the blanket. I had the other. We didn't have to sneak up on the cat. The cat saw us. It stood up. Ears flattened. Tail flicked. Head down, the cat stalked toward us with lethal grace.

"I thought that tea was supposed to make him sleepy?" Marcus said, already starting to walk backward.

I did the same. “It was supposed to. Maybe it doesn’t actually work on animals.”

“I thought you said you checked a message board.”

“I did. Just get ready to run.”

The cat growled. When he stalked closer to us, I yelled, “Now!”

The cat had slowed down. A little. Then he stopped altogether. We could hear his purring from where we sat. Evil Cat dropped his head to his paws like an all-surrender.

At first I thought maybe we’d overdone it and accidentally killed the cat, but I could see him breathing easily. We carefully wrapped the cat in the blanket and scooped him up.

He didn’t fight at all. We’d done it.

“Got you, you beast!” I muttered. Marcus stood back. I nodded at him. “Let’s get him to the vet.”

The cat wiggled in my arms on the way but didn’t try to fight me; it was almost like he was snuggling into me.

We walked back into the vet’s office and the lady behind the counter showed us into a room right away. “We’re ready this time,” she said.

I realized that everything breakable had been taken out of the room. Dr. Smith walked in and locked the door behind him. He also had a large syringe with a needle ready.

“What’s that?” Marcus asked, his eyes going wide.

“Something to settle our friend down a little. Don’t worry. He’ll wake up in about an hour.”

"Wait," Marcus said. "Jared already drugged him."

Dr. Smith frowned. "With what?"

"Calming teas," I said. "I have the packages." I nodded to Marcus and he quickly dug out the labels from the teas I used. I told the doctor what I'd done while he read the labels.

Dr. Smith did a quick calculation and took the cat out of my arms, laid him on the examination table, and injected the cat with only some of the drug in the syringe. "In the future," he said, "talk to a vet before giving animals any drugs, even the kind that aren't really harmful to humans."

"He'll be okay?" Marcus asked.

The doctor nodded. "Okay, Sparky," he said, speaking softly, "let's see who you are." He pulled out a small device that must've been a RFID reader, because he touched it to the cat's neck and a minute later a profile popped up on his computer screen. "There you go. This big guy belongs to Henrietta Duncan and his name is Puffy."

Puffy?

He tapped some keys on his keyboard and some records popped up on screen. Dr. Smith took a minute and scanned the file. "Uh-huh... just like I suspected, the poor guy has the condition I mentioned. But he was being treated before he got away which means she knows he's sick. Dr. Vespers, our other vet, had been working with her and Puffy. I'll give Ms. Duncan a call."

"Wait," Marcus and I said at the same time. I looked at him

and knew he must have had the same thought. I turned back to the doctor. "We'll deliver him."

The doctor raised an eyebrow. "Really?"

"We need to see who would own a cat like this," Marcus said. "I mean, do they live in a prison or something?"

"It's no one's fault the poor guy is sick," he said. "Poor Puffy here just needs to be contained while he's being treated. I'll call Ms. Duncan. It's not right for me to send the cat back without making sure she's aware we have him. I'm sure she's worried about his whereabouts. But I'll tell her I have a couple boys willing to deliver him." He opened the door to the waiting room. "Take a seat. As soon as I'm done I'll let you know what's going to happen."

We sat in the waiting room for the better part of an hour, wondering when Dr. Smith would come back out with the beast.

While we were waiting, the door to the clinic opened and who should walk in but Janet, cradling in her arms a small dog on a leash. She stopped as soon as she saw us.

"What are you doing here?" she asked us. Then she looked to Marcus. "I thought Penny went to Dr. Stover on the other side of town?"

What'd I say? Janet knew everything about everyone—and their pets.

"It's a little thing called doctor/patient confidentiality," I said.

"Also known as none of your business," Marcus said.

"Are you here with Penny? Or some other animal?"

"There's an animal right in front of us," Marcus whispered.

"Hmm..." Janet eyed us carefully. "You know, you two have been up to something lately. I just know it."

Just then, Dr. Smith came to meet us in the waiting room, carrying Evil Cat—*Puffy*—in the plastic animal crate.

"Ms. Duncan would be very grateful to get her cat back and it would be a big help to have him delivered back to Oak Street. Apparently he ran away a while ago, and not getting his treatment made his aggression come back."

"Cat from Oak Street?" Janet said, and I got a sick feeling in my stomach. She had that look in her eyes.

"Ms. Duncan has diffusers and medication," Dr. Smith continued. "I'm confident the cat's going to be much happier." The vet scribbled down an address on a scrap of paper and handed it to me. "Be sure to tell her to put up thicker screens to keep this bad boy inside."

"Triple screens," Marcus said.

I nodded. "Or maybe just leave the doors locked and the windows closed."

"Tell Ms. Duncan to call me if she has any questions," Dr. Smith said.

When he left, Janet was still standing there, watching us. She peered into the pet crate that held Puffy.

"You know," she said, "I heard something about a cat terrorizing that neighborhood." She stood up and looked at us.

"That wouldn't be the same cat, would it?"

"Janet, we're warning you," I said, because I couldn't think of anything else. She really was putting it all together.

She nodded her head slowly. While she stroked the top of her little dog's head, she said, "So you two goons are the ones they call the Revengers?"

"No!" Marcus and I said at the same time.

Janet smiled. "Just like I thought. Wait'll everyone at school finds out you're spending your free time wrestling sweet little baby cats."

"You can't prove anything," I said.

Janet pulled her phone out of her back pocket and quickly snapped a picture.

"Now I can." She grinned, so totally pleased with herself.

I stood up. Janet may have thought she'd gotten us, but I had something major up my sleeve. "Hey, Janet. It was so great seeing you at the mall the other day. You know, listening to Gunner Tinsdale perform?"

Her expression quickly changed from evil to dreamy. "Oh my gosh, he is like, the most awesome ever."

"I can introduce you to him," I said. "He happens to be a close family friend. All you have to do is delete that picture."

"And promise you don't spread that stupid rumor about us being Revenginators," Marcus said. I had to give it to him for purposely using the wrong word.

Janet held her phone back from us. "Why do you care about

the rumors if they're not true?"

Marcus didn't miss a beat. "Are you kidding? Whoever those guys are, they're insane. If they think we're trying to steal their glory who knows what they'll do to us."

I had to work at it not to smile.

Janet narrowed her eyes. "And you're not just messing with me about meeting Gunner, right?"

"No way," I said. "Delete the picture, and you get to meet Gunner. Simple."

"I'll tell you what," she said. "I'll delete the picture when I meet Gunner. Not before."

"Fine," I said. "But until then, you have to promise not to show anyone that picture or tell them anything you saw today." I held out my hand for the shake.

Janet looked down at my hand. Finally, she reached for it. "Deal."

We took the cat back to Ms. Duncan. She lived just a few blocks from Oak Street in a big old house that looked like ten people could live there. She almost cried when she saw her cat still asleep in the cat carrier. "Oh, Puff, you bad boy, where have you been?"

Ms. Duncan had to be eighty or more. She had that silver-gray hair that old ladies get but she had to be pretty cool because she had on tight black pants and a long red shirt with gold buttons. Gold glinted at her ears and around her neck too.

She had what Ronie would have called style, but I just thought she smelled good. Like a garden, not like an old lady.

We told her how Puffy had been roaming the Oak Street neighborhood. "You'd better keep him in. He could get hit by a car, you know," I said.

"Poor car," Marcus muttered. I shot him a look, but he gave me back an empty stare as if he hadn't said anything.

"You boys come in. You deserve a reward for bringing Puff home."

I shook my head, and Marcus said he had to get home but he couldn't remember why. We both tried to back out but she practically dragged us through the front door.

Ms. Duncan's house had little porcelain dolls on ledges and glass bells and little spoons with the flags of various countries on their handles—it seemed every surface had something breakable. She seemed to like cats, too, since she had china ones on the table and paintings of Puffy on the walls, and even cat-shaped pillows on her couch.

"It's enough that Puffy's back with you," I told her.

"No, no." She dragged Puffy out of the cat carrier. The medication Dr. Smith gave him must've been working because Puffy was totally relaxed. I was more impressed that the old woman was able to cradle the beast with one arm; she had to be stronger than she looked. Her purse sat on a thin-legged table near the door and she reached into it, muttering to herself about where had she put it? Puffy stirred and let out a sleep growl. I glanced at Marcus and we both got ready to run.

"Ah, there!" Ms. Duncan handed us twenty dollars.

"No, ma'am. We couldn't."

"Please. I wouldn't feel right."

"It'll pay for the supplies," Marcus hissed. "And more iodine."

I took the money. Ms. Duncan smiled and petted her cat. "You're such sweet boys," she said.

When the door shut behind us, Marcus let out a relieved breath.

Glancing back, I saw Ms. Duncan wave at us from the window. Puffy sat in the window, contentedly gazing out while Ms. Duncan stroked his head. He rubbed his chin against her hand, looking like a sweet cat for once. He was the picture of an angel cat.

“Better take video of that to help ease our nightmares,” I said.

“Good idea,” Marcus said, getting out the little video camera from his bag. “Also for the website. Hey, speaking of nightmares, do you think Janet will keep quiet until she meets Gunner?”

“The way she looked at him at the mall,” I said, “makes me think she will.”

Just as we turned to leave Puffy stared at us, his yellow eyes narrowed. He opened his mouth for a silent hiss. I’m no cat whisperer but it felt a lot like he was saying something—making a promise that it wasn’t over between us.

But Puffy's days of being a terror were done. His reign had been ended by the Revengers—and Dr. Smith, I suppose.

Too bad we couldn't end Gunner with a lot of calming tea and a trip home to his mom. But our success with Puffy had given me a new idea.

CHAPTER 11

We updated the Revenger website with the video of Evil Cat and ending with Puffy the docile cat. We emailed the person who'd asked for our help and told them the job was done—Evil Cat was no more. Then I explained my plan for Gunner to Marcus.

"I don't get it." Marcus sat back from his keyboard.

"You said you could manipulate the view-count on the video, right? Make it look like a ton of people had seen it?" I asked.

"Yeeeeaaaah," Marcus said. "I have the bot ready, but like I already told you, his video has thousands of hits, man. That's huge for a nobody. Even huger considering he's a nobody who butchers songs."

"The way I see it," I said, "Gunner either asked someone to record his street performance, or they did it on their own, but either way it's online. It's a train wreck, and I want that train wreck to have more views. We *need* it to have more views if our plan is going to work. I'm talking like a few hundred thousand."

"You think that'll get rid of him?" Marcus asked. "He's

going to think he's famous. He'll think he's a real rock star. He'll be even more unbearable."

"Ah, but he'll buy it when he gets a ticket to Los Angeles and a letter offering him a contract." Marcus shook his head and opened his mouth to say something. I could tell he was confused and decided to spell it out for him. "We'll fake a letter from some indie company there and say they found him online and want to hear his music in person. The Revengers will buy the ticket. Do we have enough for a one-way ticket?"

Marcus started to smile. "No, but maybe we will when the Evil Cat money comes in. And I might be able to lend the rest if we can find a cheap ticket—especially if we put him on a bus. LA's not too far away." He turned to his computer and started tapping keys. "So we give him a one-way ticket, and he's stranded in Tinsel Town playing on street corners. I like it. It's mean. Kind of ruthless, and it's going to solidify the kind of service we provide."

"You can do it?"

Marcus punched some more keys. "I've got a bot that can act like a visitor to the site. It'll hit the website and make it look like thousands love Gunner's music, or at least can't stay away from listening to him." He tapped another key dramatically. "Done. It'll take a bit of time, but it's already going. All we have to do now is send him a fake letter and buy him that one-way ticket."

A quick search made it clear that, after taxes and service

charges, the bus was the best way to go. It was affordable, and getting a ticket in someone else's name was pretty simple. We found a business letter online and copied most of it except the names. When we were done, we mailed it. Then we just had to wait and see if Gunner was dumb enough to take the bait.

We didn't have to wait long.

CHAPTER 12

"Baby, don't worry," Gunner said as Ronie drove us all to the bus station. Marcus and I had insisted we go with her. She was suspicious but let us come. "As soon as I start making that big LA money I'll send for you. I can't write beautiful words without my best girl by my side. Hey, you got any extra cash for the ride? I'll need some brain fuel when we make our stops along the road."

"Sure," Ronie said. "You know where to find it."

"Thanks, babe," he said, digging into her purse like it was his own.

I think even Ronie was tired of listening to him. She hadn't said much on the drive. She didn't need to. Gunner had done nothing but talk about this trip ever since he'd gotten the letter Marcus and I had faked.

Once we arrived at the bus station and Gunner had his guitar and one bag slung over his shoulder, Ronie just about shoved him toward security.

I'd texted Janet to meet us at the station. When I looked back toward the parking lot, I saw her running toward us.

"I'm here!" she said, waving to me. "He didn't leave, did he? I'm here!"

I waved her over.

"Okay, bye!" Ronie said to Gunner. "Text me when you get there."

Gunner looked back at her with a hint of sadness or maybe... *love* in his eyes.

"Gunner, hang on," I said as Janet joined us. Her face was flushed from running, and I was horrified to see that she'd also attempted to put some makeup on—dark pink stuff on her cheeks and light blue on her eyelids.

"Yeah, little man?" he said.

"Before you go to LA and become big and famous, I wanted you to meet one of your fans. This is Janet Everton."

"Oh my gosh it is so nice to meet you," she said. "I like, loved your playing at the mall. You are like, amazing. Like, way better than Johnny Swag, like, better than Elvis!"

Gunner's face exploded in happy grins. "Well, ain't that something?" he said. "You want an autograph?"

"Yes!" Janet said. She produced a book from her bag and a pen and handed it over to him like it was Lancelot's sword. Gunner scribbled his first autograph and handed it back to her. Janet looked like she might pass out. I did not intend to give her mouth-to-mouth if that happened.

"Stay cool," he told her. Gunner slung his guitar up higher on his shoulder and started back toward security.

"Gunner—wait!" Ronie said suddenly. "You're going to be okay, right? Your friends know you're coming?"

Gunner spread his arms wide. He still had on his ripped jeans and a faded T-shirt and, with his too-curly hair, I wished security would give him a strip search.

"Hey, babe. You're looking at the next big thing. Johnny Swag better move over." Ronie stood up on her tiptoes and kissed him goodbye. Then he turned back to me and Marcus. "Catch you later, little men." He made a fake a gun-shooting move.

"Way later," I muttered, and Marcus stifled a laugh beside me.

We managed to hold it together until Janet left and we stepped back out to the parking lot. Every time I looked at Marcus I busted up with a laugh. Marcus wasn't any better but he hid his grin behind his hand.

Before I could get into the car Ronie turned on me. "Okay. What did you do? Put itching powder in his underwear?"

"Eeeeww." Marcus wrinkled his nose. "Like we'd touch that guy's tighty-whities."

"Boxers," Ronie said. "He wears boxers."

I nearly vomited right there.

"Well, then what?" Ronie asked. "Did you replace his guitar strings with rubber bands?"

I filed that idea away. It was a bit juvenile but still pretty good. "Just happy to see Gunner so happy, you know. On his way. Like the little man said."

Marcus snickered.

Ronie glanced from me to him. "If I find out you two did anything to stand in the way of Gunner making it big, I'll—"

"Hey, we're just glad Gunner's got a chance to play his music."

"Elsewhere," Marcus whispered.

Ronie looked at us again but she let out a long breath. "Yeah, I'm not sure I could take the 'I'm Too Hot for My Own Good' song one more time."

Ronie was more than tired of Gunner if she'd actually admit that she couldn't handle endless hours of that song.

"Little man" became our password for the week on the Revengers e-mail. Ronie didn't seem too sad about Gunner not being around. He texted saying he'd arrived at his friends' place. He was going to see the indie record company the next day.

The fun lasted until Marcus called me a few days later. "Get over here fast!"

It sounded like we had a Revenger emergency. Had Janet gone back on her word? Had the site been hacked? Had Marcus's parents found out what we were doing? I made it over to his place five minutes faster than usual. His mom let me in.

"Hi, sweetie," she said, closing the door behind me. "I was just making some granola. Can I offer you a bowl?"

"No, thank you," I said.

"Well, you need some healthy energy," she said. "Take this apple instead. And you'll stay for dinner, won't you? We're have toaf-loaf for dinner—tofu meatloaf!"

"Well, I'm not sure," I said, just wanting to get to Marcus's room.

"It's really much better than you think," she said. "I like to add a little—"

"Mom! Let him go!" Marcus's voice came from his room.

"Sorry," I said to Mrs. Yardly, starting toward Marcus's room. "Better go. And thanks for the apple."

Marcus waited until I was in and had shut the door. He propped up a chair under the doorknob.

"That bad?" I asked.

Marcus pulled up YouTube. "It's not just here. It's everywhere." Gunner Tensdale's face came on the screen. He had a backup band called the Tensdale Five. Someone had talked Gunner into shaving his hair really short, and without the curls he looked older and kind of cool—if you didn't know what a jerk he was. The logo for the indie record company we had used for our fake letter came up.

"No way!" I sat down with a thud on Marcus's bed.

"Way. Gunner must have used that letter we sent him to talk his way into getting them to really listen to his music. But listen up." Marcus turned up the sound on his computer as Gunner started singing a song about skinny girls. *I'm so fine, you're mine. I'm too hot for songs that don't rhyme. Take a look at my face, la la la ohhh.* But Gunner no longer sounded like someone letting the air out of a balloon. Someone had put his voice through Auto-Tune and probably a few other mixers to sweeten the sound and prop up his vocals. With someone else playing the guitar, Gunner sounded a lot like a genuine pop star. Marcus hit mute and pointed to the screen. "Look at the views."

Three million.

My throat tightened and I had to cough to clear my throat. "And that's not the video your bots were working on, right?"

"No. But that one has close to three million views too."

I met Marcus's stare. "What have we done?"

CHAPTER 13

"You know, Daisy, I just want to make awesome music. For the fans. They're what really matters because they're like, the reason I'm here."

We watched with our jaws hanging open as Gunner was interviewed by an entertainment reporter. The story was called "Busker Makes it Big." His fame had spread like a California wildfire.

One minute it was only online, the next thing we knew his song was on the radio and the local newspaper was running full-page stories about him. I'm sure his fame was confined to local sources, but it felt like he was everywhere.

"That's so wonderful," the blue-eyed reporter said to him. She gazed at him like he really was the next Johnny Swag. Geez, he just might be. Which kind of made us want to barf. "Now, can you answer one very important question? Are you single? I'm only asking because the fans want to know."

"Ah, Daisy," Gunner said, with mock humility. "You're going to get it out of me one way or the other, aren't you? Well, yes, there is a girl in my life. Her name is Ronie, and she's the only person who ever believed in me. She's the reason I made it this far."

"I'm gonna barf," I said once the interview was over and Marcus had turned off his computer.

"I can't believe we actually sort of did it," Marcus said. "Not like we thought we would but... the plan did work."

"True," I said. "Gunner is gone. I wonder if Ronie has seen this yet. She's been bragging to anyone who will listen that his song is on the radio."

"Let's go to your place and find out."

At home, we found Ronie watching the interview on a loop, over and over again. By her side she had an envelope.

"Look," she said, holding up the letter. "You two nerds always tried to tell me that Gunner was a loser but he always kept his word. Look what he's done."

She thrust the papers at us, and I took them. I couldn't believe what I was seeing. Gunner had sent her a check with all the money he'd ever borrowed from her, and then some. He wrote that he wanted her to concentrate on her gymnastics and sign up for classes with that fancy Russian coach she'd always talked about.

"I can't believe he actually did this," I said.

"I told you so," Ronie said. Her phone signaled a text, and her face lit up. "Gunner says the view from the Hollywood sign is beautiful," she said, reading the text. "He's about to send a picture."

As bizarre as it was, Ronie and Gunner actually seemed to be closer now that there was distance between them. I wondered if maybe it was because she could convince herself she was dating the guy on TV and not the real Gunner. I guess there was a chance the guy had changed, but that was slim. Either way, Ronie seemed to love having a musician boyfriend who was now really hot. She became the envy of all her girlfriends, and I think she liked texting Gunner instead of having him over at the house every day. She got to walk around like she was majorly connected, and Gunner sent her a copy of his new single that he dedicated to her. "My Sweet Saltine" may turn out to be a one-hit wonder, but so far it hasn't faded away. How could it, with brilliant lyrics like this:

When you're sweet
You're like candy
But sometimes you're salt
Like a big ol' meanie
But you're my
Meanie
Baby
You're sweet

Ronie was happy enough that she even ruffled my hair one day. I told her not to even think about doing that again. She gave me an evil smile and called me her "little man." I told her I'd put her toothbrush in the toilet if she said it again. Things were back to normal after that.

Sky seemed happier, too, since she could sit in the kitchen and eat a PB&J without Gunner looming, or without him having eaten all the PB and the J before she could get to them. I was just happier in general. Ronie wasn't on my case so much, taking out her frustrations with Gunner on me. And no one other than her was calling me "little man."

That just left Marcus.

He sulked around for three days and wouldn't even go to the skate park to burn off some steam. I finally cornered him after school. "What is your problem?"

"Problem?" He glanced around to see who might hear but the teachers had already gone home for the day and Janet was out sick. He stepped closer. "My problem is that we're supposed to be Revengers. That means we're supposed to be tough and scary and dangerous. That means like ninja kind of cool. But look how we started off."

"What are you talking about?" I asked.

"We found a lost cat and transformed a jerk into a pop star."

I shrugged. "So?"

"So?" Marcus threw his arms out to the side. "So it's not exactly the stuff that puts the fear of god into the hearts of our enemies, is it? I don't want the Revengers to be a team that helps people by doing good deeds."

He had a point. "Okay. From now on, we're going to be scarier."

"Promise?"

"Black shirts all the way. In fact, I think we should tweak the website a bit. Make it so it looks like we *took out* Evil Cat. And I'm not sure how to make what we did to Gunner look scary, but we can at least say we took out a jerk. As long as people don't know it's *the* Gunner Tensdale."

He scuffed a toe into the dirt. "Okay. I think I have a plan for that."

Marcus came through. He manipulated a few video clips of Evil Cat and put together a montage showing what we'd done to take out Gunner. He showed a picture of Gunner with black Xs over his eyes, then showed him getting on the bus and driving off. Next he showed shots of a quiet, event-less home with us sitting around happily playing board games. Of course, Marcus pixelated our faces so you couldn't tell who it was. In the end it made for a pretty scary video, since we took out an actual person. It would be great for business, I was sure of it.

A few days later the website started getting a lot of hits. Payment came in from the Evil Cat job and we had offers from all over the place. Everyone wanted their sisters' jerky boyfriends taken out or some bully dealt with. Our spy camp money was growing.

Even though the online form we created was designed to look like people could make requests to us anonymously, they weren't. Marcus made it so we could track the source of any request. Barely a day after word started spreading about our website we had a request from my own house. Ronie.

Or at least, I assumed it was. The request read, "Aaron Jefferies called me a snob. Do me a favor and send him to the Amazon jungle."

Marcus and I had a good laugh about that one. And even though we were probably going to ignore most of the requests since we wanted to choose our jobs very carefully, the fact that our business was getting some attention made us feel incredible.

We had a new slogan too:

The Revengers: Give us a name and one way or another, that person (or animal) will never bother you again.

Keep reading for a Sneak Peek

at BOOK #2

in the

REVENGER SERIES

CHAPTER 1

The gun felt slick in my hands. Cold. But a comfortable cold. It belonged in my hands. I peeked around the corner to look for my target. No sign of him. A can rattled behind the concrete pillar to my right. I stepped out. The hairs on the back of my neck tingled. Something wasn't right. I turned and spotted movement. A shadow. Marcus darted out from a shelter behind me. I raised the end of my gun and shot first. Marcus fell to the ground in a dramatic death.

Then he looked up. "I still nailed you three to two."

I shot him again. Paint exploded over his chest in another splat of blue.

He raised his gun and fired two shots that exploded against my chest. I was about to return fire again when he raised his hands. "Okay, okay, enough. Truce!"

I nodded and lowered my gun and smiled. "You're supposed to yell HIT when you get hit, remember?"

He crawled back to his feet and rubbed the spot where I'd hit him. "Ow! Next time I'm wearing three sweaters under this." He tugged at his dark coveralls with the PAINT DEATH logo on the shoulder. "But you saw me get hit," he said, poking me in the chest. "And you know it's against the rules to shoot a man while he's down."

I shrugged. "Revengers play by their own rules."

He laughed and put his arms out to the side. "You really think this helps us? I mean, we're Revengers, not assassins. We're not killers." He pulled off his goggles and wiped the sweat out of his eyes.

"We need all the skills we can get—and that includes sharpening our stalking skills." I glanced up at the sky. "We should get back."

I figured we had about an hour left of sunlight. We'd started coming to the paintball park after school every Tuesday and Thursday. I'd told Marcus we needed killer instincts if we were going to stay in the Revenger business. But he was right. We didn't really kill people. We made problems disappear. Sometimes those problems were people. Other times, like our first job, those problems were animals. Specifically, a beast we called Evil Cat who terrorized a nearby neighborhood. We trapped the cat, took him to the vet for treatment, and safely delivered him back home to his thankful owner. The neighborhood's problem did disappear, but in the end it felt more like a good deed than true Revenger business.

"It's working," I told him, as we stripped out of our protective gear. "We're sharper."

"Whatever you say." Marcus groaned and then said, "Dude, my mom is going to kill me if I come home with blue all over this shirt. It's new."

The coveralls stopped most of the paint, but if you got shot around the neck or right on the zipper the way Marcus had, the paint got through. He had blue marks on his shirt.

"It'll wash out. And your mom won't even notice. But you can come home with me and wash it there if you're worried."

"Nah, I should be okay."

That was obvious. Marcus's parents were pretty cool about whatever Marcus was into. Only-child syndrome, he called it. When you're the only child the attention is all on you so you get more attention than kids from bigger families—at least that's what Marcus said. I had two sisters so maybe my parents split their attention between us, but then I had two more people watching my every move. I was pretty sure I had more attention, not less.

I followed Marcus out of the park. "Listen, I'm not kidding. I really think coming here and practicing this stuff is helping us. It's sharpening our senses." I waved at the park. "I could feel you sneaking up on me."

Marcus snorted. He stuffed his hands in his jeans pockets. He'd been my best friend since forever. He was also my partner-in-not-so-much-crime and the mastermind behind our website.

"We need another really good request to come in," I said. "Something to push our business over the next hump. We're not getting the kind of requests I want us to get. Nothing super challenging. I'm worried we're going to get rusty."

"That reminds me," Marcus said. "I gotta go home and check the email. We can't afford to crash the server again or my dad's going to start asking questions about how much traffic we're getting. Besides, it hasn't been that long since we had a good target walk into our sights. What about Pant-Crapper?"

I smiled. We'd taken on a few nothing jobs since we launched our business. A couple bullies in neighboring schools were no longer bothering their classmates. Pant-Crapper—the guy Marcus was talking about—was one job I had been happy to take on. He was the kind of bully you read about in the newspapers. He beat up kids, stole from them, scared them, made life in the halls a living nightmare for that school. We actually received more than one request for help dealing with this one guy.

It was a pretty good job, but as good as it felt to get rid of him, it really had been too easy. It took us all of three days to come up with a plan for the bully and an afternoon to implement it.

We started by writing his name on the elastic band of a bunch of tighty-whitey underwear—big capital letters in felt pen. Full name, even his middle name so there was no mistaking who the underwear belonged to. Then we strategically put melted chocolate on them so it looked like the guy crapped his pants... all the time. Then we left them all over the school. We taped them to his locker, hung them from the basketball nets, scattered them in high-traffic areas of the school, and even put a couple pairs on the desks of teachers whose classes he had.

It was effective. Ruthless, by some standards, but not the challenge I was looking for.

"We have an awesome site," Marcus said. "We're building a reputation. As long as we keep our eyes and ears open, that next big job will come along. It'll probably just step right into our path. It'll be so obvious we won't be able to avoid it if we try."

Turned out Marcus was totally right. The following day we—the Revengers—were given the opportunity of a lifetime.

CHAPTER 2

I'd stayed up all night working on my history assignment. I was exhausted but confident. And when the classroom door opened I expected to see Ms. Blindly. Ms. Blindly was a total rock star, one of those teachers who really understands her students. There wasn't a kid in the entire school who didn't love her. One of the reasons I'd done my homework was because I didn't want to disappoint her.

But when I saw the man who walked into the class—the man we all knew too well—I joined with the rest of my class as we released a collective groan.

Mr. Shevchenko smiled when he heard it. It was such an awkward name we all called him "Mr. Shev" but not to his face. That he fed off the misery of his students was only one of the many rumors about this substitute teacher. Some of the others had him hanging around retirement homes at night and mugging the elderly. Or that he was one of America's most wanted criminals and had been hiding out as a lowly middle school sub for the last few years, biding his time before he went on another crime spree. My personal favorite was that instead of milk on his morning cereal, he used the tears of orphans. Honestly, all of those could have been true. It might also have been true, however, that he was just a jerk who loved giving out detentions.

"Good morning, class." Mr. Shev's accent always reminded me of someone trying to fake it as a vampire from an old movie. It made my skin crawl. Going by the shivers of everyone around me, I wasn't the only one. "As you may have guessed, Ms. Blindly will not be here today, or—" He licked his lips, pausing for a moment before finishing his sentence, "—for the rest of the week."

Marcus dropped his head onto his desk, and a second groan rose up around me.

"There is even a possibility," he added, "she will be gone for the rest of the semester."

From her front row, center seat, Janet Everton, who had to know everything about everyone, asked, "Is she sick? I hadn't heard anything like that. Was she in an accident? Is she okay?"

Mr. Shev stepped so close to her desk she had to crane her neck back to see his face.

He cleared his throat. "Ms....?"

"Everton. Janet Everton."

Shevchenko nodded. "Well, Ms. Everton, you have earned yourself two afternoons of detention."

It was as if Mr. Shev had just said something to Janet in Japanese, or Swahili, or some other foreign language. She blinked at him. "Pardon me?"

"Detention, Ms. Everton. You will report here at the end of school today, and tomorrow as well."

She shook her head. "I don't understand."

"Well, then three days ought to give you plenty of time to figure it out. You've earned another day for yourself. Congratulations."

Realization settled on Janet. Her shoulders slumped like a deflating balloon. "You mean just because I asked if Ms. Blindly was okay?"

"Because you spoke without first raising your hand." He pointed at her. "Which you have done yet again, and so you are now up to four days of detention. Speak again and you'll have the full week."

Janet didn't get in trouble... ever. Not by Ms. Blindly. Not by any other substitute teacher we'd ever had. In fact, in the dozen or so times we'd had Mr. Shevchenko I couldn't remember him punishing her. Which was probably why he didn't know her name.

From the back of the room I could see her ears redden. It must've taken all her effort but she kept her mouth shut. Janet wouldn't cry. She'd go out at recess and stomp around, shout about it, maybe even kick a tree or something, but she didn't go in for tears.

"I think I have a candidate for our next target," Marcus whispered to me.

"Marcus Yardley," Mr. Shev called from the front of the room. "I know your name. Thank you for speaking out of turn. You and your partner in crime will get to join Ms. Everton for the first day of her detention."

"Partner in crime?" Marcus asked.

Putting up my hand and waving it, I told him, "I didn't say a word."

Shevchenko clapped his hands together and rubbed them. "This is marvelous. The two of you just earned four days in detention. At least Ms. Everton won't be lonely." He cast his gaze around the room. "Anyone else want to join them?"

Marcus glanced at me with his mouth hanging open. I shook my head and mouthed, "Don't speak." Turning to the front of the room, Mr. Shev glared at me.

"Something you want to add, Mr. Moter?"

I shook my head. I didn't say a word. But what I wanted to say was, "Alex Shevchenko, prepare to meet the Revengers."

CHAPTER 3

By lunch seven of us had been scheduled for detention and by the end of the day that had risen to twelve. When the last bell rang only a little over half the class left. Those who did ran for the exit as if zombies had just come in through the windows.

Mr. Shev sat on the edge of Ms. Blindly's desk and shook his head at the twelve who remained. "I'm disappointed in all of you. I know it's common practice to give the substitute teacher a hard time, but I thought we," he gestured to himself and then to the rest of us in a sweeping motion that reminded me of a ringmaster, "were different. I thought you saw me as something more than just a substitute." He tsked and added, "I think maybe you've all just forgotten how much history we've had together." He clapped his hands and stood. "Pull out a pen and paper. You can leave detention as soon as you write out your first memory of me. When do you recall first having me as a teacher? I think writing it out would be helpful in reminding yourself that I've been part of your educational experience for quite some time. You will each read your work aloud before you leave."

Everyone started muttering to each other and more than one person said, “What is he talking about?”

He snapped his fingers and cast a glare around the room. I pulled out a sheet of paper.

The first memory I had of Mr. Shevchenko came from first grade. He’d been a substitute for Mrs. Meister. During lunch—which we ate at our desks—I remembered him wandering the room, plucking items from our lunch bags and eating them. I had a piece of strawberry fruit leather I’d been saving until the end of my lunch. It was my favorite back then—still is—and he walked up and took it off my desk as if stealing food was totally allowed. He didn’t even try to hide what he’d done.

I wanted to write that out. I wanted him to know that he wasn’t at all respected and that pretty much everyone hated him. But I needed to be smart. I needed to think like a Revenger. If I was going to take the man out of commission, I needed to stay off his radar.

The only problem was, I didn’t have a plan yet—except to avoid more detention.

In the end I wrote about how he’d helped direct a Christmas concert during second grade. He’d talked about how he nearly became a famous stage actor, but decided to be a substitute instead. Even at seven years old I knew how ridiculous that was. Worse than his bragging was the way he’d talked to the cast as if we were not very good Broadway veterans. He told one kid he looked constipated when he sang, and another that her voice had the squeaking quality of a caffeine-addicted chimpanzee—whatever that meant. Both kids went home crying more than once, but Mr. Shev didn't notice or didn't care.

Still, I left those things out of my paper and kept the focus on his fantasy of his own brilliance.

"Ah yes," he said when I'd finished reading my paragraph to the class. "I played Othello in college, you know. I'd only been in the country for a couple years—having arrived from Ukraine as I might have mentioned."

He had mentioned it. Multiple times.

"My English wasn't perfect at the time," he continued.

"Still isn't," Marcus whispered.

I coughed to cover up my laugh and Shev glared at me before continuing. "I even had a bit of an accent. Probably hard to believe hearing me talk now. But I landed the lead in a Shakespeare play. I had a promising career ahead of myself. But alas..." Standing, he looked up at the ceiling. "I felt a calling to work with children and mold youth into our future leaders."

"And we're so grateful." I had to consciously stop myself from rolling my eyes.

"Any chance you'll be heading back to the Ukraine to visit anytime soon?" Marcus asked.

Shev's eyes narrowed. "I haven't seen my family in years, but I hope I'll be able to go there soon. I'd love to reconnect with them."

He seemed almost sad about it, but Shev was heartless,

and I was pretty sure you needed a heart to be sad.

He called on the next student and one by one everyone else shared uninteresting stories of Shevchenko subbing for various subjects and teachers. Most were half-true and watered down so Mr. Shev didn't get angry. Marissa Lewis talked about how in the fourth grade she was impressed with how Mr. Shev had kept control of some of the kids by making them write sentences over and over. But I remembered that day. I'd been one of the kids writing sentences. What Marissa had left out was the fact that our sentences had to say, "I will not speak out in Mr. Shevchenko's class because he is the greatest teacher on the planet and we love him." It had been infuriating.

I glared at him. I was going to be smart about this. I'd stay off his radar. But payback was coming, Mr. Shev.

Turning to Marcus, Shevchenko said, "And finally, Mr. Yardly, would you please share what you remember about our first meeting?"

Marcus cleared his throat. I knew that what he was about to say wouldn't be helpful to our mission. I tried to give him various eye signals to warn him, but he didn't see me. I was pretty sure I looked like I was having a massive face spasm.

"In third grade," Marcus began, "you were the substitute for Mrs. Tan's class the week after Halloween."

Mr. Shev nodded as if he remembered the time well. But I knew where this was going and it was nowhere good. I cleared my throat, shifted in my seat, stretched my arms above my head—anything to grab Marcus's attention. Nothing worked. I didn't even attract Mr. Shev's attention; he was so caught up in his own memories.

"I remember," Marcus continued, "because I had brought two mini chocolate bars from my trick-or-treating. I was saving them for after lunch, but before I could even take the first bite of my PB&J, you came by and snatched the chocolate from my desk and ate it. Right in front of everyone." He looked up and eyed Shevchenko, who had stopped nodding and stared at my friend with narrowed eyes and a clenched jaw.

"I think you have me mistaken for another teacher," Shevchenko said.

"No, it was you. But don't worry, I don't look at it like you stole from me. I look at it like you saved me from getting a cavity." Marcus smiled. "So thank you so much."

No one in the room moved a muscle. I'm pretty sure we all couldn't believe what we were seeing. Marcus held his ground, smiling at Shevchenko like he was a sweet old man. Shevchenko, on the other hand, looked like he was about to explode.

Slowly, and some would say bravely, Janet raised her hand.

"Yes?" Shevchenko asked, without looking away from Marcus. "What is it, Ms. Everton?"

"Well, um, I was just wondering." She wet her lips and coughed, and it was clear that even someone as brave as Janet felt a little intimidated by Mr. Shev. "What I mean is, I think I speak for everyone when I say we're really happy you're here."

Shevchenko turned to Janet with a raised eyebrow. She plowed forward like a soldier heading into battle without a gun. "I think we're all curious about the health of Ms. Blindly. Is she in the hospital? Or out of town? How is it possible she'll be gone all semester?"

It had to be driving Janet bat-crazy not knowing what was going on with Ms. Blindly. Mr. Shev knew it as well, or seemed to. But I had a feeling he was underestimating the resources Janet had at her disposal. If he didn't tell her, she'd find out another way. Janet knew people all over town and she wasn't afraid to talk to them. She regularly babysat for Ms. Abrahams, the school office secretary. Janet's mom worked at the most popular hair salon in town, which practically every woman in town visited at some point. Janet often helped out there, and from what I heard from my mom, the gossip was as easy to get as sand at the beach.

Still, Mr. Shev seemed determined to keep Janet in the dark as long as possible. Probably just because he was mean like that. "I'm not at liberty to pass it along to a bunch of children. Just know that you and your classmates will be in my capable hands."

He nodded at the clock. "You've all been here long enough today." He seemed to be telling us to go, and Marcus and Andrew Levi stood to go. He raised an eyebrow and smiled at Marcus. "I didn't dismiss you yet. You two have another day's detention. That's the whole week for you, Mr. Yardly. Congratulations."

Marcus smiled and bowed before plopping back in his chair.

"You're all dismissed," Shevchenko said.

Storm clouds rolled overhead as we walked home. Sky went home with one of her friends from school so we didn't have to walk her. Grayness seemed to permeate the street and the cookie-cutter homes we passed along the way. But my mood probably had something to do with that. Marcus spoke when we were a few blocks from the school. "Tell me you have a plan. That guy is an even bigger jerk than I remembered."

I shook my head. "I don't have a plan yet, but it's forming. I can feel it. I need more time. What about you? Any ideas?

"Several. I say we slowly make him go insane—or at least make him think he's gone insane. We could create some sort of water leak right over his desk—slow dripping, all day long. Oh! Or we could make him think he's gone deaf. You know, we could all pretend to be talking but not really make a sound. If we play our cards right he might end up in the super crazy ward in the hospital. In one of those little padded rooms in a straitjacket." He laughed. "I'd pay money to see that."

"Yeah," I said, thinking over his ideas. They were crazy, all right. "But if we can pull off getting rid of a teacher, our Revenger reputation would be concrete. Imagine all the kids willing to throw their allowances at us to take their teachers out of commission for a few days."

"If we're going to pull that off, we better have a killer plan for how to get rid of Shev. Something that drops people's jaws when they hear about it. Plus, it'll have to be totally clear that we were responsible."

"The Revengers," I said. "Not us specifically—the Revengers need to get the credit."

"That's what I meant," Marcus said. He snapped his fingers. "Oh, what about this?" He turned to face me, walking backwards. "Hide his keys in his shoes. Or put dog turds in the pockets of his jacket? Break into his house and put double of everything he has in his fridge so he thinks he bought everything twice. I mean, that would totally make a guy go crazy."

"Not a bad idea, but it's not big enough. Besides, I don't think we want to break and enter this early on."

"We need to be ruthless," Marcus said. "I'm sick of people emailing the Revengers asking us to turn them into rock stars."

I groaned at that. My sister's jerk boyfriend had been one of our first targets as Revengers. He was a loser who treated me and my sister like garbage. We manipulated an online video of him singing on the street and made it look like he had thousands of fans. Then we tricked him into leaving the city, to no longer bother me and Ronie. It all worked like we'd planned, except that he ended up landing a recording contract and was now climbing the charts.

"You're right. We'll hit Shev with everything we've got. Show the world what the Revengers are really made of. He's the perfect target too, since he thinks he can treat us any way he wants and there's nothing we can do about it." I clenched my fists. “I mean, he ate your candy! What grown person eats a kid’s candy?”

“A crazy one,” Marcus agreed.

“Okay, here’s what I think. We need it to be very clear that the Revengers are taking Shev down. So I say we private message the whole class—everyone including ourselves—and say that The Revengers have been commissioned to take out Mr. Shev. Make sure that tip button is extra big so they can donate when we succeed.”

“There might be a few who rat us out, you know.”

I shook my head. “They’ll rat out the Revengers. I don’t care about that. I don’t care if Shev knows he’s a marked guy. As long as they can’t trace it back to us, we’re gold.”

Marcus nodded excitedly. “Awesome. I can’t wait. So, can I assume you have a plan brewing in that head of yours?”

“Yeah, I have something brewing.”

“Well, what is it? Are you going to somehow get the guy fired?”

“Nah,” I said, starting to smile. “Something even better.”

READ THE SERIES
BE PART OF THE MAYHEM!

If you liked this book,
check out these other books
by STEVEN WHIBLEY

Made in the USA
Middletown, DE
05 July 2018